Biscuit Crumbs

For Daisy

First published in the UK in 2005 by
QED Publishing
A Quarto Group company
226 City Road
London EC1V 2TT
www.qed-publishing.co.uk

A Catalogue record for this book is available from the British Library.

ISBN 1 84538 179 3

Written by Brian Moses
Designed by Alix Wood
Editor Hannah Ray
Illustrated by Francesca D'Ottavi – EDI

Series Consultant Anne Faundez
Publisher Steve Evans
Creative Director Louise Morley
Editorial Manager Jean Coppendale

Printed and bound in China

QED Write On

Biscuit Crumbs

Brian Moses

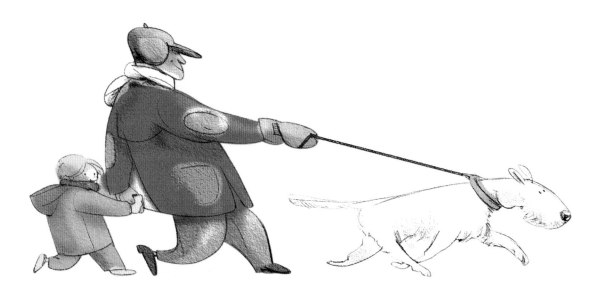

QED Publishing

Are We Nearly There Yet?

When we went on holiday this year
my little sister just wouldn't be quiet.

Again and again
she kept on asking,
"Are we nearly there yet?"

We drove to the end of our street
and my sister said,
"Are we nearly there yet?"

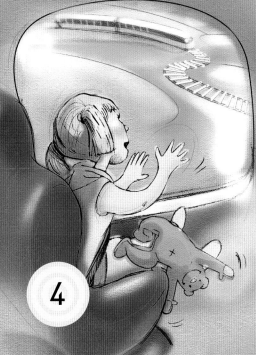

We left the town behind
and again she said,
"Are we nearly there yet?"

We stopped for a train to go by
and my sister called,
"Are we nearly there yet?"

4

We sped along the motorway
and my sister said,
"Are we nearly there yet?"

We stopped for something to eat
and my sister grumbled,
"Are we nearly there yet?"

We waited in a queue of cars
and my sister screamed,
"ARE WE NEARLY THERE YET?"

We caught a glimpse of the sea
and my sister yawned,
"Are we nearly there yet?"

But when we finally reached the end
of our long and tiring trip,
my sister didn't say anything,
she was fast asleep ... zzzzzzzz!

5

At the Playground

When we went to the playground
I swung on the swings,
I slid on the slide,
I hung from the rings.
I raced over to Mum
for a kiss and a cuddle,
but as we were leaving,
I fell in a puddle!

I-am-a-ro-bot

I-am-a-ro-bot
and-all-that-I-say
will-be-spo-ken-to-oth-ers
in-this-ro-bot-way.

I'll-hum-and-I'll-buzz
as-I'm-cross-ing-the-floor,
then-I'll-bleep-bleep-bleep-bleep
till-you-o-pen-the-door ...

7

Biscuit Crumbs

"Don't eat biscuits at night
or you'll get biscuit crumbs in bed."
That was my dad's advice
and I wish I'd listened to what he said.

I thought that I knew better of course,
and the jammy dodgers were yummy,
but now it makes no difference if I lie
on my back or on my tummy,

**because I'm itching, I'm twitching,
I'm tossing and turning all night.
I'm lifting the covers and shifting about
but nothing makes it right.**

These biscuit crumbs keep troubling me,
keeping me wide awake
and I'm brushing them like crazy
while giving the sheets a shake.

And I wish I hadn't eaten them now,
I wish my bed was clear.
I wish I had a magic spell
to make them disappear,

because I'm itching, I'm twitching,
I'm tossing and turning all night.
I'm lifting the covers and shifting about
but nothing makes it right.

And I'll never eat biscuits in bed again,
well, not till tomorrow night!

9

Big Ted

Big Ted is fun to have around,
he's a really big-hearted bear.
I've loved him ever since the day
Dad won him at the fair.

If I bump Big Ted down the stairs
he never seems to worry,
he doesn't complain or make a fuss
or tell me I'll be sorry.

The smile upon his face
never seems to disappear.
He didn't even frown or wince
when Mum re-stitched his ear.

Big Ted worries about me
when I'm at school each day –
will I dress up warm enough
when I'm sent out to play?

He mothers me when Mum's
                          not there,
he understands when I'm sad,
he's never grumpy or sharp with me
and nothing makes him mad.

I'm almost as tall as him now,
but no matter how much I grow,
Big Ted is a special friend to me
and always will be, I know.

Creepy House

Creepy house,
creepy house,

I hate living in
a creepy house,

with squeaking doors
and creaking floors,
with bats and rats
and noisy cats.

This really is
an awful place,
In every mirror
I see a face,

but it isn't mine,
this face I see,
and I'd give anything
not to be

in a creepy house,
a creepy house.

I hate living in
a creepy house.

Walking the Dog

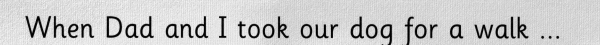

When Dad and I took our dog for a walk ...

He chased a fat cat over a log,
he barked and barked at a jumping frog.

He opened his mouth and caught a fly,
he lay on his back and stared at the sky.

He licked my ice-cream when I wasn't
                                    looking,
he sniffed the smell of pies that were
                                    cooking.

He wanted to come on the slide with us,
he howled and made such a terrible fuss.

Then he rolled in something that smelled really bad
so I walked ahead and left him with Dad.

And after our walk, which had taken an hour ...

Our dog had a bath ...

and then gave us a shower!

You Can't Catch Me

"You can't catch me," my sister said.
"I bet you I can."

So I chased her, round the sofa,
under the table and into the playhouse,
between the chair legs
and out into the garden.

We ran twice round the fish pond
and then … I lost her…

"WHERE ARE YOU?"

"GOT YOU!"

The Goldfish's Dream

I'm a nothing special fish
floating about all day.
I open and close my mouth
and I don't have a lot to say.
But I have a special dream,
a dream that's really nice.
I dream that I'm an angel fish
swimming in paradise!

My Face

I can see my face
smiling back at me
from the shiny bauble
on the Christmas tree,

from the mirror on the wall,
from the kitchen kettle,
in knives and in forks
I see me in the metal.

I stare at my face
in cars that I pass,
in silver foil,
in polished glass.

One side of a spoon
finds me upside down
but right side up
when I turn it round.

In a puddle or pond
I'll find myself there.
Some days I seem
to be everywhere.

19

What do you think?

Read the poem 'Are We Nearly There Yet?'
Have you been on a long journey? How did you feel?

Can you find the two pairs of words that rhyme in the poem 'At the Playground'?

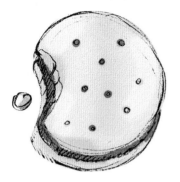

Do biscuit crumbs make your bed itchy? What is your favourite type of biscuit?

Read the poem 'Big Ted'. Do you have a soft toy that's a really special friend?

21

What sort of creatures would you find in a creepy house? What sort of noises would you hear?

Read the poem 'Walking the Dog'. Do you have a pet? Is your pet naughty?

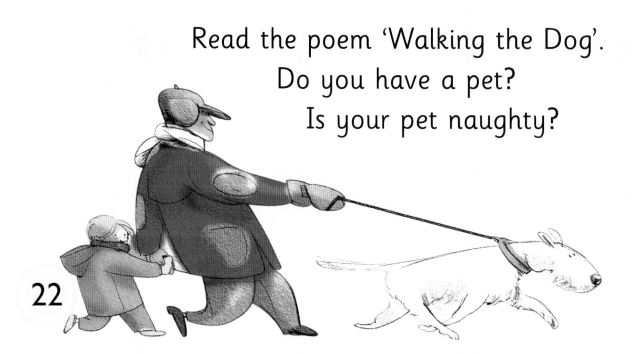

22

Read 'The Goldfish's Dream'. Can you think of another dream that the goldfish might have?

When you have read 'My Face', try to find other things that act like mirrors.

Parents' and teachers' notes

- Talk to your child about his or her experience of journeys. Is 'Are We Nearly There Yet?' something that your child says, too? Together, make up an additional verse to the poem. For example, 'We waited at traffic lights/ and my sister yelled/ Are we nearly there yet?'

- Look at the poem 'At the Playground'. Read it with your child and decide how you are going to say the last line. Will it be said sorrowfully or in a jokey way? Can you think of a different disaster for the last line?

- Read 'I-am-a-rob-ot' in a robotic voice. Talk about what the robot might look like. Can your child draw the robot? Then, talk about what else the robot might do and add a further verse to the poem. For example: 'I'll-cook-you-some-lunch/ then-I'll-clean-up-the-house/ but-when-I'm-switched-off/ I'll-be-quiet-as-a- … '. What will the last rhyme be?

- Read 'Biscuit Crumbs' to your child. Talk about the rhyming sounds in the poem. Can your child pick out the words that rhyme in each verse?

- Read the poem 'Big Ted'. Can your child identify the pairs of rhyming words? Re-read the poem, omitting the second word of each rhyming pair. Can your child remember the missing words?

- Together, read 'Creepy House'. Can your child think of spooky sounds to go with a reading of the poem? Once you have experimented with different sound effects, you could record the result and discuss whether or not it works. How could you improve it?

- Read 'Walking the Dog' and suggest that your child draws a picture to accompany his or her favourite line. Ask why this line is his or her favourite.

- 'You Can't Catch Me' is a poem that doesn't rhyme. Suggest that your child draws this poem in a sequence of pictures (i.e. round the sofa, under the table, into the playhouse, between the chair legs, etc.). Then, discuss what's happening in each picture. Can your child find the other poem in the book that doesn't rhyme?

- Read 'The Goldfish's Dream'. What does an angel fish look like? Help your child to research this fish, in books or on the Internet, to discover some facts about it.

- Read 'My Face' and ask your child if he or she can think of reflective surfaces that are not in the poem. You could walk round your house/school and try to spot shiny surfaces. Make a list of them and then try to compose an additional verse for the poem.